Published in the United States by Random House Children's Books,
a division of Random House, Inc., New York.
Originally published by Random House Children's Books in 1960.

Beginner Books, Random House, and the Random House colophon
are registered trademarks of Random House, Inc.
THE CAT IN THE HAT logo ® and © Dr. Seuss Enterprises, L.P. 1957,
renewed 1986. All rights reserved.

Visit us on the Web!
www.randomhouse.com/kids
www.seussville.com

Educators and librarians, for a variety of teaching tools, visit us at
www.randomhouse.com/teachers

Library of Congress Cataloging-in-Publication Data
Geisel, Theodor Seuss, Green eggs and ham, by Dr. Seuss [pseud.] New York,
Beginner Books: distributed by Random House, 1960.
62 p.   illus.   24 cm.   (Beginner books, B-16)
I. Title.   PZ8.3.G276Gr   60-13493
ISBN 978-0-394-80016-5 (trade) — ISBN 978-0-394-90016-2 (lib. bdg.)

Printed in the United States of America

83

Green Eggs and Ham

By Dr. Seuss

BEGINNER BOOKS
A Division of Random House, Inc.

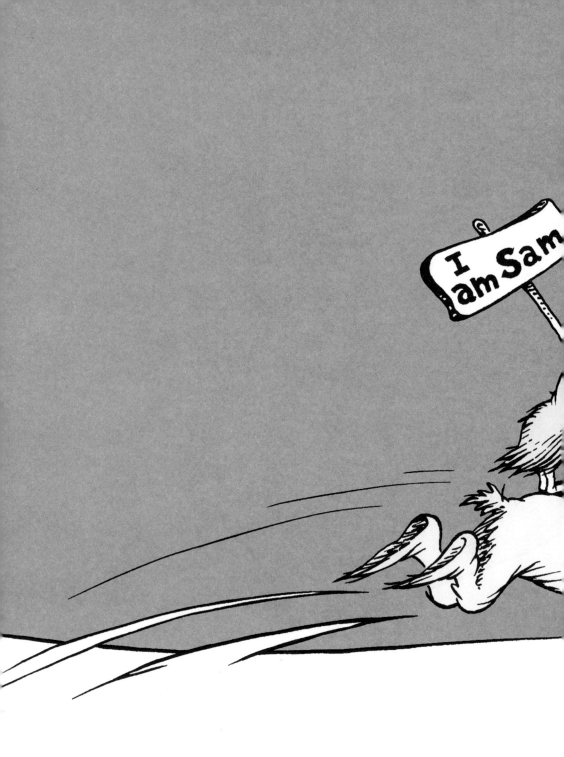

That Sam-I-am!

That Sam-I-am!

I do not like

that Sam-I-am!

Do you like
green eggs and ham?

I do not like them,
Sam-I-am.
I do not like
green eggs and ham.

13

Would you like them
here or there?

I would not like them
here or there.
I would not like them
anywhere.
I do not like
green eggs and ham.
I do not like them,
Sam-I-am.

Would you like them
in a house?
Would you like them
with a mouse?

I do not like them
in a house.
I do not like them
with a mouse.
I do not like them
here or there.
I do not like them
anywhere.
I do not like green eggs and ham.
I do not like them, Sam-I-am.

Would you eat them
in a box?
Would you eat them
with a fox?

Not in a box.

Not with a fox.

Not in a house.

Not with a mouse.

I would not eat them here or there.

I would not eat them anywhere.

I would not eat green eggs and ham.

I do not like them, Sam-I-am.

Would you? Could you?
In a car?
Eat them! Eat them!
Here they are.

I would not,
could not,
in a car.

You may like them.
You will see.
You may like them
in a tree!

I would not, could not, in a tree.
Not in a car! You let me be.

I do not like them in a box.

I do not like them with a fox.

I do not like them in a house.

I do not like them with a mouse.

I do not like them here or there.

I do not like them anywhere.

I do not like green eggs and ham.

I do not like them, Sam-I-am.

A train! A train!
A train! A train!
Could you, would you,
on a train?

Not on a train! Not in a tree!

Not in a car! Sam! Let me be!

I would not, could not, in a box.

I could not, would not, with a fox.

I will not eat them with a mouse.

I will not eat them in a house.

I will not eat them here or there.

I will not eat them anywhere.

I do not eat green eggs and ham.

I do not like them, Sam-I-am.

Say!

In the dark?

Here in the dark!

Would you, could you, in the dark?

I would not, could not,
in the dark.

Would you, could you,
in the rain?

I would not, could not, in the rain.

Not in the dark. Not on a train.

Not in a car. Not in a tree.

I do not like them, Sam, you see.

Not in a house. Not in a box.

Not with a mouse. Not with a fox.

I will not eat them here or there.

I do not like them anywhere!

You do not like
green eggs and ham?

I do not
like them,
Sam-I-am.

Could you, would you,
with a goat?

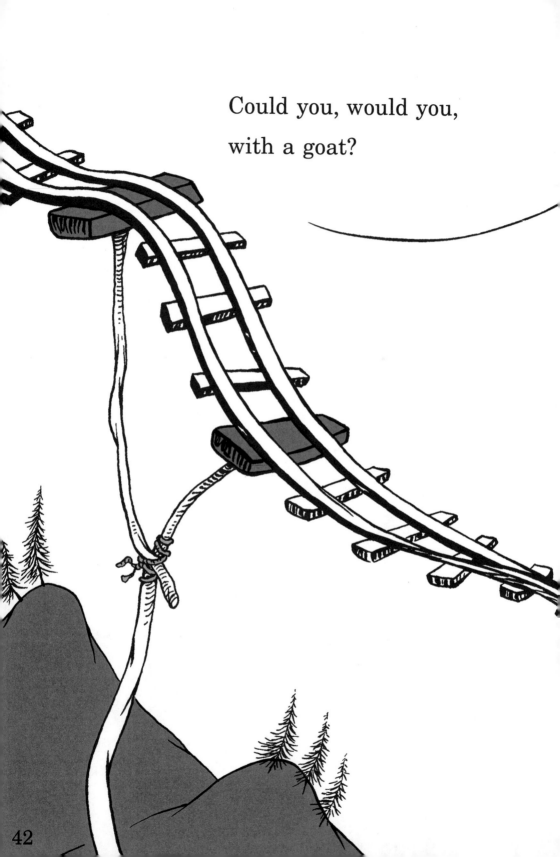

I would not,
could not,
with a goat!

Would you, could you,
on a boat?

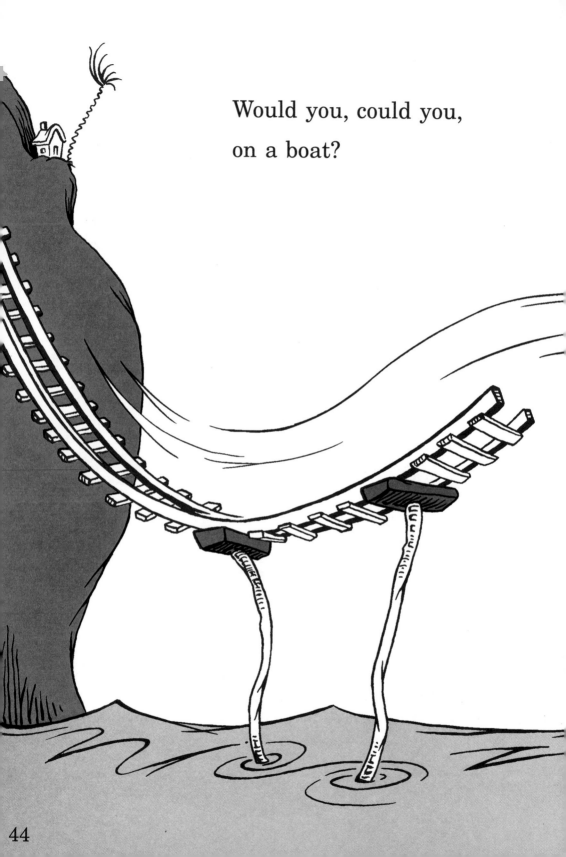

44

I could not, would not, on a boat.

I will not, will not, with a goat.

I will not eat them in the rain.

I will not eat them on a train.

Not in the dark! Not in a tree!

Not in a car! You let me be!

I do not like them in a box.

I do not like them with a fox.

I will not eat them in a house.

I do not like them with a mouse.

I do not like them here or there.

I do not like them ANYWHERE!

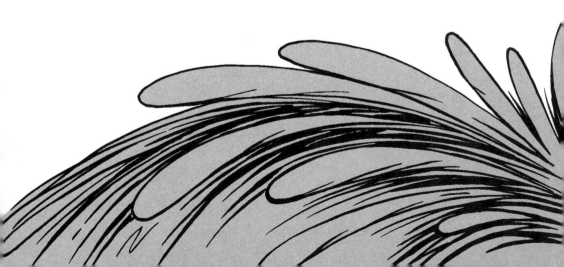

I do not like
green eggs
and ham!

I do not like them,
Sam-I-am.

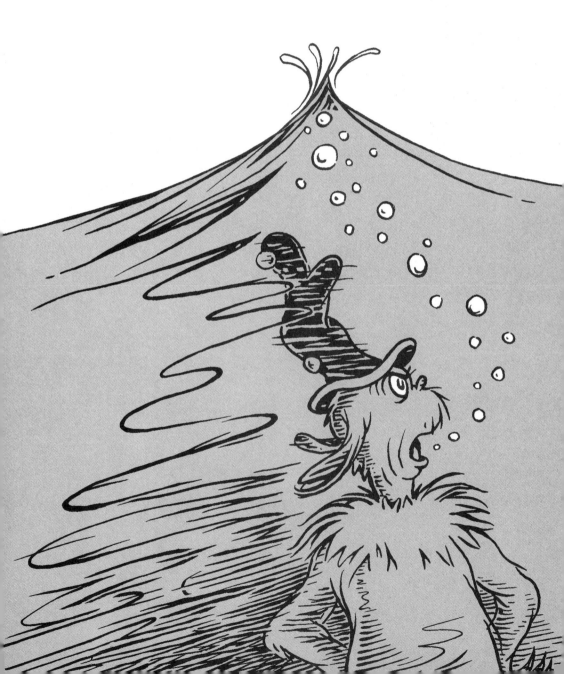

You do not like them.

So you say.

Try them! Try them!

And you may.

Try them and you may, I say.

Sam!

If you will let me be,

I will try them.

You will see.

Say!

I like green eggs and ham!

I do! I like them, Sam-I-am!

And I would eat them in a boat.

And I would eat them with a goat . . .

And I will eat them in the rain.

And in the dark. And on a train.

And in a car. And in a tree.

They are so good, so good, you see!

So I will eat them in a box.

And I will eat them with a fox.

And I will eat them in a house.

And I will eat them with a mouse.

And I will eat them here and there.

Say! I will eat them ANYWHERE!

I do so like
green eggs and ham!
Thank you!
Thank you,
Sam-I-am!